Llyfrgell Sir POWYS County Library
Llandrindod Wells LD1 5LD
www.powys.gov.uk/libraries

LIBREX-

Books are to be returned on or before
the last date below.

Rhaid dychwelyd y llyfr hwn erbyn y dyddiad diwethaf a stampiwyd uchod.

A charge will be made for any lost, damaged or overdue books.
Codir tâl os bydd llyfr wedi ei golli neu ei ni weidio neu heb ei ddychwelyd
mewn pryd.

on

978 1 4451 1812 3 pb

978 1 4451 1811 6 pb

978 1 4451 1813 0 pb

hic fiction

978 1 4451 1799 7 pb

978 1 4451 1801 7 pb

978 1 4451 1800 0 pb

-fiction

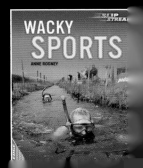

FISHING FOR TROUBLE

DAVID AND HELEN ORME
Illustrated by WARREN PLEECE

EDGE
W FRANKLIN WATTS

LONDON·SYDNEY

First published in 2013 by
Franklin Watts
338 Euston Road
London NW1 3BH

Franklin Watts Australia
Level 17/207 Kent Street
Sydney NSW 2000

A CIP catalogue record for this book is
available from the British Library.

ISBN 978 1 4451 1812 3

Series Editors: Adrian Cole and Jackie Hamley
Series Advisors: Diana Bentley and Dee Reid
Series Designer: Peter Scoulding

1 3 5 7 9 10 8 6 4 2

Printed in China

Franklin Watts is a division of
Hachette Children's Books,
an Hachette UK company.
www.hachette.co.uk

CONTENTS

CHAPTER 1
ADAM'S HUGE FISH

Will and Adam went fishing every weekend.

It kept them out of trouble.

There were lots of gangs on their estate.

Will always caught a fish, but Adam never did.

As usual, Will soon felt a tug on his line.

"Awesome!" he yelled.

Adam was annoyed. He hadn't caught anything.

Then he felt a tug on his line.

"I've got one now!" he shouted.

"And it's huge!"

Adam pulled and pulled. Up came an old tyre!

Will tried not to laugh.

CHAPTER 2
ADAM'S NEXT CATCH

Adam soon felt something else on his line.

Something really heavy.

"Bet it's another tyre!" laughed Will.

But it wasn't. It was a bag.

Someone was hiding in the bushes.

He was watching Will and Adam.

He was furious that they had found the bag,

because he had hidden it there. He had come

back to get it.

CHAPTER 3
RUN FOR IT!

Will opened the bag.

"Wow!" he said.

The bag was full of jewellery.

Then they looked at each other

in horror.

"Oh no!" said Adam. "It was on TV! That biker gang robbed a jeweller's shop!"

"What are we going to do?" whispered Will. "If anyone knows we've found this, we're dead!"

They ran off before anyone could catch

them. They left behind their fishing gear

and the bag.

CHAPTER 4
TO CATCH A THIEF

The man in the bushes rushed out to grab the bag. He didn't see Will's fishing line. He tripped over the rod and fell head first into the river. Then his arm got tangled up in Adam's line. The bag was lashed tightly to his arm.

This time, the man was being watched from

the bushes.

"Quick, Adam, call the police!" whispered Will.

The man came up, spluttering. But the bank

was slippery and he couldn't climb out.

CHAPTER 5
LOST REWARDS

Two police officers were quickly at the scene.

They pulled the jewel thief out of the river.

"I wonder who called us?" said the first officer.

"They never gave a name," said the second officer.

"Shame," said the first officer. "They can't collect the reward. Could have been the best day's fishing they ever had!"

VAMPIRES ARE
SO BORING

DAVID AND HELEN ORME

EDGE

In a lonely churchyard, a vampire wakes.
He must find food... human blood.

Two girls find him – they want him to be their
boyfriend like the vampire off the telly.
But the vampire has other ideas...

EDGE
FRANKLIN
WATTS

LONDON•SYDNEY

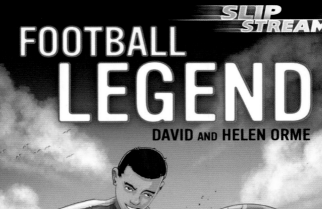

SLIP STREAM

FOOTBALL
LEGEND

DAVID AND HELEN ORME

EDGE

Rob is always being picked on by Martin.
This time, it's for hanging out with his granddad.

But with the school football trials looming, perhaps hanging out
with Granddad isn't such a bad idea...

LONDON•SYDNEY

FOR TEACHERS

About

SLIPSTREAM

Slipstream is a series of expertly levelled books designed for pupils who are struggling with reading. Its unique three-strand approach through fiction, graphic fiction and non-fiction gives pupils a rich reading experience that will accelerate their progress and close the reading gap.

At the heart of every Slipstream fiction book is a great story. Easily accessible words and phrases ensure that pupils both decode and comprehend, and the high interest stories really engage older struggling readers.

Whether you're using Slipstream Level 2 for Guided Reading or as an independent read, here are some suggestions:

1. Make each reading session successful. Talk about the text before the pupil starts reading. Introduce any unfamiliar vocabulary.

2. Encourage the pupil to talk about the book using a range of open questions. For example, what treasure would they most like to find?

Slipstream Level 2 photocopiable **WORKBOOK** *ISBN: 978 1 4451 1797 3 available – download free sample worksheets from: www.franklinwatts.co.uk*

3. Discuss the differences between reading fiction, graphic fiction and non-fiction. What do they prefer?

For guidance, SLIPSTREAM Level 2 – Fishing for Trouble has been approximately measured to:

National Curriculum Level: 2b
Reading Age: 7.6–8.0
Book Band: Purple

ATOS: 2.1*
Guided Reading Level: I
Lexile® Measure (confirmed): 320L

*Please check actual Accelerated Reader™ book level and quiz availability at www.arbookfind.co.uk